GOOD MONSTERS AND FRIENDS

stories

MERC FENN WOLFMOOR

ROBOT DINOSAUR PRESS

Robot Dinosaur Press

www.robotdinosaurpress.com

GOOD MONSTERS AND FRIENDS: STORIES

ISBN: 978-1-949936-44-5 (ebook)

ISBN: 978-1-949936-45-2 (paperback)

Cover & interior design by Bog Wolf Cover Designs

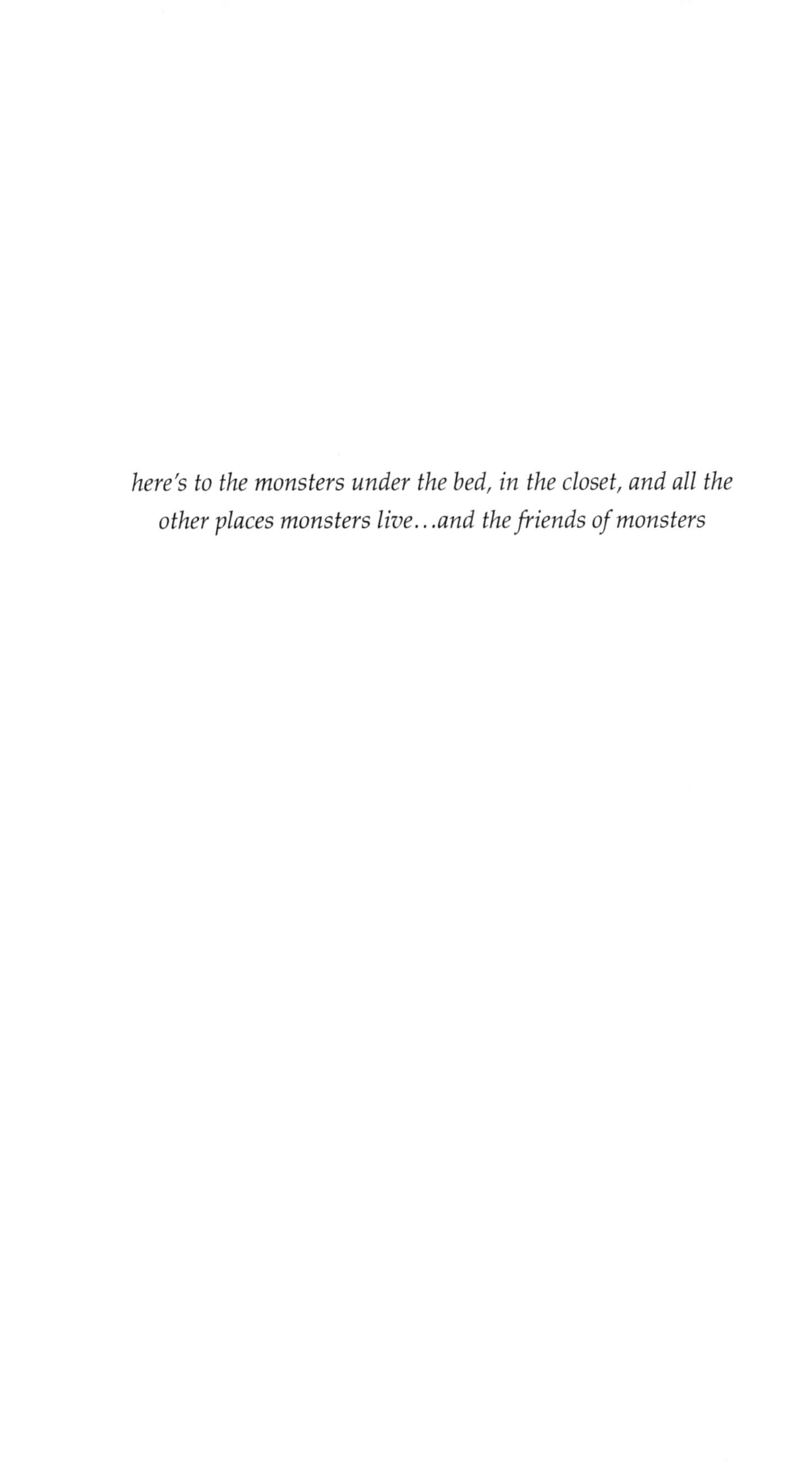

here's to the monsters under the bed, in the closet, and all the other places monsters live…and the friends of monsters

CONTENTS

INTRODUCTION

Most of these little stories (tweetfics) came about through prompts: I would ask people to choose a theme/word/color/etc and I would write them a tiny story that fit (usually) in a tweet. I've expanded and edited a few of them for this book. It was always a blast to write micro fiction for people, and I thought, well, some of my favorite little pieces ought to be collected somewhere, you know?

So what better place than a new short story collection!

There are a handful of longer stories as well, including a brand new flash story, "Eternal Paper Birds." This one came about when I was listening to an audiobook and learned about the Oscar Wilde story called "The Nightingale and the Rose" (which you can read for free online if you want to get mad about it, like me). It pissed me off to the extent I had to immediately thrown down a gauntlet—er, that is, write something in response.

The last tale in this collection is my Nebula Award

finalist story, "This Is Not A Wardrobe Door," was also inspired by being mad about classic literature. In this case, Narnia. I'm *still* mad about Susan's treatment, portal fantasy's obsession with coming back to the Real World and abandoning the magic (or yourself), and I will not forgive Lewis for that utterly bullshit Revelations-esque ending in *The Last Battle.* Anyway! I obviously have a Lot Of Feelings about certain children's books, and I'm extremely proud of "This Is Not A Wardrobe Door" and I hope you, too, feel empowered to make your own doors, and your own choices.

I hope you enjoy these tiny stories of friendship and exploration, fairy tales and spaceships, dinosaurs and robots. I wish you all the best in your adventures here in our world and in any portal you venture through.

—Merc Fenn Wolfmoor
    May 2022

GOOD MONSTERS AND FRIENDS

JUST LIKE MOMBEAST USED TO MAKE

"I brought cookies," Kyli says as she crawls under the bed. "It's all we have left in the cupboard."

Bisq, the pink puffy monster who lives under her bed, sniffs and wipes their face with an oversized claw. "Not hungry."

Disappointed, Kyli sets the paper plate of Oreos down in the dust anyway. "Okay."

Outside, the holes in the house let in cold air and the crunchy sounds of bigger, more bad monsters skulking around. Skulk is a word Kyli learned from Bisq and she impressed Ms. Jenny at school by saying it.

Kyli and Bisq lie on their tummies. The bed smells like dryer fresheners. Mom always washed her blankets on Tuesdays. (On Tuesdays, Kyli takes Bisq to the closet so Mom won't find them.) Mom is outside right now, with her guns, fighting the bad monsters that want to eat everything.

"I'm scared," Bisq says.

"No one can get us in here." Kyli pats Bisq's hand. Bisq's fur is always full of static, and sometimes they jump on the bed with the lights out to make electricity shoot out from Bisq's fingers. That always makes Kyli laugh. "It's okay."

"What if your mama shoves all the others back through the rift and then finds me?"

Kyli frowns. She knows about the rift, because Mom explained it. That's where all the monsters came from— especially the bad ones. The good monsters asked to come in first, like Bisq. "I'll tell her you're good," Kyli says.

"Tell me what?"

Mom's voice is suddenly right there, right outside the edge of the bed. Bisq squeaks and Kyli gasps. She shoves the cookies towards Bisq and pokes her head out to see. "Nothing, Mommy."

Mom's covered in sooty black dust that comes when bad monsters are pulled through the rift—maybe helped by Mom's guns. She folds her arms, her pistols holstered at her sides.

"Nothing, huh?"

Kyli tries to look as honest as she can, because Mom says that honest people are good, and she wants to be good like Bisq. "I'm—"

But Mom yanks the covers off the bed and flips the mattress up so fast it's like in a movie and she has superpowers. Bisq clutches the plate of cookies and peers up at Mom, their eyestalks and tails trembling with fright.

"Thought as much," Mom says, her face getting dangerous. "Always suspected one of you snuck in and made an anchor point for the rest."

"Mommy, this is Bisq and they are my friend!" Kyli grins, hoping that Mom will not look so mad.

"Monsters are not friends," Mom snaps.

"Yes, they are," Kyli says. She crawls back under the frame and wraps her arms around Bisq. "See?"

"Get back here right now," Mom says in her Angry Voice.

Kyli should listen. That's what good girls do. But if she lets go of Bisq, she's afraid Mom will send them away. "No," she says. "Not until you promise not to hurt Bisq."

Mom's face flushes. That's a word Ms. Jenny taught Kyli. "No, Kylinne."

Bisq doesn't cry the way people cry, but they try to become a very small monster. Kyli's eyes start making tears for them both. "Don't send Bisq away! We haven't even had cookies yet!"

Mom's mouth opens, and then she stares at the plate Bisq is holding. "You brought Oreos?"

"So we could have a snack." Kyli sniffs. "You're always busy shooting bad things. I'm hungry."

"I'll go away if you want," Bisq says in a squeaky voice. "Just...don't be mad at Kyli, okay? She's really nice. And good."

Mom's face starts to look normal—tired, but not mad. "I..."

Kyli takes three cookies from the plate. She hands one to her mom, one to Bisq, and keeps one for herself. "Ms. Jenny says everyone makes bad decisions when they're hungry, Mommy. Eat a cookie first before you do anything bad."

Mom's legs seem to bend like playdough and she sits

down. She rubs her face, then looks at the cookie. "One snack," she says. "Then we'll talk."

Kyli nods. She smiles at Bisq, who slowly sits up next to her. "It'll be okay," she whispers.

Quietly, all three of them take bites of their cookies. Kylie's is a little crumbly on the outside, but the frosting is delicious. She wishes she brought milk, which would make the snack even more better.

"These taste just like my mombeast used to make!" Bisq says, smiling. Crumbs speckle their pink fur. Then Bisq looks sad again. "Mombeast got kicked out and I don't know where she is..."

Kyli pats Bisq's hand again. "Maybe we can find her after snack. I'll help you look."

Mom looks away.

Kyli and Bisq finish their cookies. "Can Bisq stay?" Kylie asks, now that none of them are hungry and won't make bad decisions. "They don't have anywhere else to go. And we can have sleepovers every night! Then I'm not scared of the dark."

"I...think that would be okay," Mom says slowly. "If your friend stays." She swallows, looking at her guns. "Maybe we need to exchange more cookies and less bullets, huh?"

Kyli nods solemnly. Cookies are always good. Then she gives her mom a hug.

Bisq eats the rest of the cookies, smiling through crumbs, and eventually, Mom smiles back and hugs Kyli tight.

BEST MONSTERS

"All the best monsters are purple," says the blobby purple sphere.

"Not true," replies the squiggly orb. "Some are green."

"No!" shouts the blustering square. "They are blue!"

In the corner, the tiny pink monster drooped and shriveled. No one ever picked its color as the best.

Suddenly, a child crawled under the bed. All the monsters froze, waiting to see who would be picked to be the One.

The blue monster swelled. The purple monster puffed. The green monster undulated.

"Pink is my favorite color!" the child said, and the little monster beamed.

GOLD

Day 13: we've struck gold! praise be!

Day 14: something's odd bout this vein. light keeps twisting off it, turning aquamarine at the corner of yer eye

day 15: we done mined that vein til only rock's left behind. we're rich!

day: aw damn, there's a dragon lying behind the gold.

MAIZE

The homeowner scowled. "This isn't what I ordered."

The designed glared back over the rows of corn. "You said you wanted a garden of maize. I got it for you!"

"I said I wanted a garden *maze*!"

"Oh…well, we can fix that. Corn mazes are popular this time of year."

OPPERTUNITY

It's dark. Colder for longer. At least when her battery quits, she has the song—her last received message.

Death is lonely.

Then, suddenly, warmth. Light. Oppy's sensors come online. A human smiles at her.

"Hey, buddy. I'm sorry it took us so long to come get you. But you're home now."

BAD, BAD BLACK SHEEP

They say messenger sparrows can find any location exactly if they study a map. I don't believe everything I hear. It'd be an occupational hazard if I did, given how many folks have tried to trick me, set me up, or scam me into climbing giant beanstalks like my cousin was a couple years ago.

After crashing into the wall on either side of the window, the sparrow made it through and wobbled to a stop on the kitchen table. Then it fell beak-first into my coffee. I sighed.

I set the sparrow carefully to the side of my mug and extracted the tiny message scroll from its leg. It swooned and collapsed. I smelled pumpkin beer—no wonder it couldn't find the window.

The message was simple:

> Help me! In jail.
> —Baa Black Sheep

I dashed to the closet and pulled on my trench coat. What had Baa gotten himself into now? It couldn't be good. We're buddies, and he never asks for help unless it's bad. I mean, really bad, not just price hikes on shears and burlap wool-carrying bags.

I locked up—padlocks, a few hexes, and the anti-reporter wards—set the sparrow on the front step to recover, and walked briskly towards the town hall/jail.

"Read all about the murders." Simon the paperboy sounded far less enthusiastic about his job than normal. "All the juicy details here." He limpidly waved a copy of the Goosetown Daily Times and Rhymes around.

"I'll take one," I said.

Simon scowled and shoved the paper at me. I'd caught him breaking parole, stealing pies from pie carts, and I'd gotten him sentenced to community service all year.

"What, ain't you read it yet, *detective*?"

"Ain't a detective," I said. "I'm a private investigator. Were you eating pumpkin pie?" I resisted adding "stolen" to that.

He scowled deeper. "Beer, and you damn well better remember I'm old enough."

"Long as you stay away from the pies."

I unfolded the paper. I don't like anything delivered to my door after the incident a couple years ago. The ex-king Cole (before he'd been deposed by his daughter) hadn't liked how I'd handled his giant infestation, and he'd sent me a nettle-bomb. It hadn't been pretty. I still have scars.

The headlines blared out at me in homicidal bold type. I was going to file a complaint.

MASTER, DAME, BOY—FOUND DEAD.

No rhymes. That reeked of non-professionalism in this town. Frowning, I stepped out of the middle of the road and scanned the front-page story.

Last night, Master Shepherd of Wool Fancies, Inc. was found murdered from suffocation in a bag of black wool. In a shocking discovery, Shepherd's mistress—Dame Bo Peep—was found dead in the exact same fashion.

Early this morning their son, the boy down the lane, was found by his sweetheart. The boy had also been murdered from wool immersion.

Police have the prime suspect in custody. Mr. Baa Black Sheep, an employee of Shepherd, was last seen delivering the wool to the three victims hours before they were murdered. According to the police reports, all the killings took place during the great Pumpkin Gala hosted last night.

It was serious if the Pumpkin Gala reports had been shoved to the second page.

Baa wasn't the kind of guy to murder people, especially in his own wool. No, not that I thought he was a murderer, but still. In wool? That screamed "hate crime."

The story went on:

---

*"I didn't do it," says Black Sheep. "The Master and the
Dame were always good to me. They bought whole bags of
wool even in this market." No witnesses claim to have
seen Black Sheep the night of the murders.*

I shoved the paper in my pocket and started walking.
No one got falsely blamed for a crime and punished for it
in my town. Especially not a buddy like Baa. I know what
it's like to get the rap for something that isn't your fault.

Hell, back when I was a kid, a bunch of old women
blamed me for killing seven giants and I ended up running
for my life from the Guild of Giants for years.

At the jail, I nodded to Wolf the bailiff. He wagged his
tail and buzzed me into the cellblock.

"Mornin', Jack."

"Morning, Wolf," I said. "Can I talk to Black Sheep?"

"Don't know why you bother," Wolf said. "Seems like a
straightforward homicide."

"You're one to talk." I popped a stick of gum into my
mouth to help keep the smell of pumpkin at bay. Wolf was
a heavy drinker but he got over it fast. His breath, not so
much. "That deal with the Swine Brothers last fall,
remember?"

"Don't remind me." Wolf growled and rolled his eyes. "I
still say it's pretty clear the sheep did it this time."

"So what's the motive?" I handed over my pistol and let
Wolf pat me down and sniff for narcotics. He freelanced as
a nose-for-hire in drugs cases all over the countryside.
Goosetown ain't exactly a high crime rate per capita place.

"Money?" Wolf nodded that I was clean. "Bunch was

missing from the scene. I also hear that the Dame kept turning off his advances so he killed them all."

"Uh huh. Look, I'll get to the bottom of this. Let's keep the speculation to ourselves."

Wolf stayed back and I sauntered down the cool brick hall. At the end of the cellblock, I stopped and stared at Black Sheep, who sat huddled in orange coveralls, shackles on his legs.

"Hey, Baa."

He looked up. "Oh, hi, Jack."

"Want to tell me what happened?"

He blinked hard. "Not my fault. I'd never hurt them!"

"Calm down, buddy. Tell me where you were last night."

"I had to work late. I delivered some bags of wool—"

"To all three victims?"

Baa nodded miserably. "It was the usual quota. One for the Master, the Dame, and their boy down the lane. I didn't want to stay up too late at the Gala since I worked in the morning, so I got some pumpkin beer and went home. Quiet party by myself, you know?"

I nodded, smelling the fermented pumpkin on his breath. The gum wasn't helping, so I popped it out and mashed it onto one of the bars. "Go on."

"So I had a few drinks and went to bed. Next thing I know, Wolf puffs down my door and drags me here saying I'm guilty of murder!" Baa snuffled and blinked his soulful eyes. "I swear I didn't kill anyone, Jack."

"Did you talk with anyone else?"

He rubbed his nose. "Just that reporter. Luis Nimble."

I sighed. "Do I have to remind everyone not to talk to the press?"

Baa shrugged. "You think maybe it was a butler?"

I held up a hand. "Never blame the butlers. They got unionized recently, and their PR gal is touchy over the subject."

Baa propped his chin on his front hooves. "I don't want to go to the shoe factory in Cross Bun, Jack! Who'll take care of my cousin Ba?"

Damn. I winced when I remembered the little gray sheep in the next town over, to whom Black Sheep sent part of his monthly earnings. Ba was working hard to pay off his medical bills after he'd lost the lawsuit against the barber who had almost killed him in a shaving "accident." Long story short, the barber had better lawyers. Baa was helping his cousin get out of debt.

Together they were just managing.

"I'll get this sorted out," I told Baa.

I marched out and went looking for the reporter.

It wasn't hard to find Luis Nimble. He'd made his name (which he'd changed from Jack, seeing how many Jacks there were at the time) jumping candlesticks as a boy, but now middle age had caught up with him and he didn't do shows any more. Now he was trying to make his fame and fortune as a freelance reporter.

It hadn't been going so well up until now.

He sat in the deli across from the town hall, at one of the outdoor tables, basking in the fact his story had made page one. He hadn't changed. Still wore his fleecy coat and wool cap that hid his balding pate, and he'd over-done the aftershave or something because he was a walking advertisement for Pines in Summer scent.

I slid into a chair across from him, ordered a stiff drink—coffee, black—and gave him a disarming smile. "Hey, Luis."

He smirked. "And you said I'd never make it big time, Jack."

"Guess you proved me wrong."

"It'll be the first time of many."

"Uh huh. So how'd you get the scoop? I thought everyone was covering the Pumpkin Gala."

Luis snorted and picked some gray-black lint off his jacket. "And compete with every wannabe rhymester and reporter in town? I'm an inventive guy, Jack. I hit the streets looking for the darker side—the stuff that happens when the candles go out."

I sipped my coffee. "And you found Master Shepherd dead, is that it?"

"If only! No, I got a call from Miss Muffet—she's in homicide now, did you hear? Anyway, she'd been doing the beat for Wolf so he could go to the Gala, and was heading past Master Shepherd's house and had this hunch, you know? Ever since the spider incident, she's been super alert and she tells me something didn't feel right. No lights, no music, no nothing. So she goes over and snoops around and hears a struggle. Goes around back and finds Master Shepherd dead. She saw a sheep hurrying off—"

"I didn't read that in your story," I said.

Luis waved that off. "Oh, it's in the official report. Got to save some juicy bits for the trial report, eh, Jack?" He winked at me.

I turned my mug of coffee in both hands. Usually Luis

wasn't this chatty but I guess excitement had gone to his head. And he was trying to lord it over me, prove he'd gotten the big story and had all but brought in the perp. Unlike me, who'd just heard about it this morning.

"Muffet called it in and got me the tip, but she didn't catch the sheep. So she goes over to warn Dame Bo Peep, but she's dead too. Ditto their boy, Little Blue."

"Pays to have friends on the force, I suppose."

"Wolf's old school," Luis said. "Muffet's the one to have on your side, the up-and-coming type with a career to make."

"Like you."

"Yup. Now if you'll excuse me, Jack, I'm going to turn in my evening edition story." He smirked, slapped a bill on the table to cover my tab, and swaggered off.

I sipped my coffee and picked up the bill.

It was one of the older fives, with Cole's face on it. Huh. I didn't think they circulated these any more. Some people kept them as souvenirs—like the late Shepherd and Dame Bo Peep—but it was bad taste to use them anymore. I bet he'd done it just to get on my nerves, given my history with Cole.

I frowned. Luis had never been the sort to save money, let alone keep it long enough that it was several years out of circulation. I pocketed it and replaced it for a couple of ones with governor Goldilocks on it. Her juvie record for breaking and entering hadn't dimmed her charisma, and she'd won the general election last year in a landslide.

I jogged over to the jail and looked for Miss Muffet. She was covering for Wolf while he was on coffee break. She wore a pinched-lipped expression like it was the next fashion about to sweep the nation.

"Prisoner's off limits until the trail this afternoon," Muffet said.

"That's fine. I was wondering if I could ask you a few questions."

She sighed and tightened the elastic band that held her golden curls in a rigid ponytail. "You turn reporter, Jack?"

"No, but I don't take everything Nimble says at face value."

Muffet grimaced, pulled out a smoke, and lit up. "Yeah, I got him the tip, though how the hell he got there so fast, I dunno. I don't like the little candle-hopper, but he'd said last week if I kept him in the loop he'd do some coverage for me, give me some good PR once he broke in big time." She took a drag. "I figured what the hell. Who'd have ever thought Nimble would make it?"

"Did you see the perp fleeing the scene?"

"Think so."

"A sheep?"

Her scowl deepened. "Bull. Not a bull literally—"

I smirked. "I know what you mean."

"Did Nimble tell you that? About me seeing the perp?"

I nodded.

"Damn, I told him to keep it out of the papers."

"He did that much. What did you see?"

"I saw something but I couldn't tell what it was. It might have been a sheep or someone in a jacket. It's cold out this time of year." She shrugged. "We got the wool connection and the fact Black Sheep wasn't at the Gala and Wolf made a guess and brought him in."

"Seems a little premature."

"Baa's no longer in the Union, and he's the most plausible suspect."

"Shepherd was no lightweight and Bo Peep was a black belt." I scratched my chin. "Think a drunken sheep could take them out?"

Muffet crushed out the cigarette on the overfilled ashtray. "No, but both of 'em trusted sheep. They wouldn't get suspicious until it was too late. And they know everyone in town so it's not like they had much to worry about. Dame got clubbed over the head before being suffocated, and Master Shepherd was pretty drunk himself."

"You had a couple?"

She snorted and I smelled pumpkin again. Damn, I was getting sick of pumpkin.

"After my shift. I needed it by then. Who *wasn't* drinking last night?"

Good point. I'd stuck to rye beer (ain't too fond of the pumpkin stuff after one batch had some coach polish in it and I found out the plant was recycling transformed fruit illegally) but I'd had a few slices of Mrs. Shoe's famous pumpkin cobbler.

"Anything else odd about the crime scenes?" I asked. "Prints? Trace evidence?"

"Wolf sniffed it out but whoever it was wore some heavy cologne to hide the scent. And he was gloved." Muffet shrugged. She wore a thin flannel over shirt that didn't hide her shoulder rig. "Bo Peep's crook—you know, the old one she broke beating the crap out of her flock the one time they lost their tails?"

"Hard to forget that." The story had been all over the papers for weeks and Bo Peep had officially retired from shepherding after that due to pressure from the union for Sheep and Shepherds.

"It turned up missing, and a bunch of cash was stolen from Master Shepherd's place. Bunch of the collectible stuff. I guess Cole is paying through the nose to get all his bills back."

I fished through my pocket. "You mean ones like this?" I held up the five with Cole's face grinning merrily at us printed on it.

She snatched it. "Where the hell you get this, Jack?"

"Luis Nimble."

"Wait a minute…"

Our eyes met and suspicions clicked at the same time. Muffet ain't a slowpoke.

"Grab Wolf and come on," I said. "Black Sheep didn't do it. "

"Luis, that flea-bitten sneaky rat!"

"Don't libel the rats," I warned her. "Pied Piper, Inc. has a hell of a team of lawyers."

She ran back to grab Wolf from the break room.

I bounded down the steps and back into the brisk October chill.

A few minutes later, my lungs burning from the run, I caught up to Luis Nimble outside the paper's main office. I grabbed him by the collar and slammed him into the wall.

"Fess up, Nimble." I gave him my best nasty glare.

"What the hell is this!" Luis shoved me in the chest.

He'd been working out—he was stronger than I remembered and I fell back a step. He pulled his cap down harder over his ears.

Behind me, Wolf and Muffet loped up.

"Arrest him for assault," Luis demanded. "First giants, now reporters. Oh, you're really moving up in the world, Jack."

"Shut up and talk."

Wolf's deep voice was more a growl than words. "We're waitin'."

Luis sneered. "I'm about to turn in my evening edition story." He reached into his pocket and brought out a folded sheaf of papers. "You have no reason to hold me, so back off. All of you, before I spread the word about police brutality."

"Is this wool on your jacket, Luis?" I reached over and plucked a curl of black-gray lint off his coat. I rubbed it between my fingers. "Kind of like what Black Sheep always sells, huh?"

Muffet and Wolf flanked him on either side.

"I never let you on the crime scene," Muffet said.

"Mind turning your jacket inside out, Luis?"

"Why?" His eyes narrowed.

"I think you got it renovated to look like a sheep pelt."

"Get real, Jack."

"This is how I see it, Luis. You needed that break or you were going to have to look for work out of town. Shepherd wouldn't hire you after you tried to scam him with that automatic candle lighter a few years back. The Pumpkin Gala was your big opening: everyone would be drunk and partying."

Sweat dripped down his face. He folded his arms.

I leaned closer. "You didn't like Shepherd and Dame Bo Peep, and their kid was just an easy target. You could knock 'em off, blame Baa for it—him being the perfect fall guy—and make your career with the story."

"You can't prove this."

"You weren't drinking last night, were you?"

Luis shifted uneasily. "What does that have to do with anything?"

"Well," I said, smelling normal bad breath and too much cologne on him, "seems to me that you'd need to be pretty sober to take on Bo Peep and wrestle down someone like Master Shepherd. And Muffet says that the perp she saw could have been a sheep or some guy in a jacket. How'd you get to the scene so fast?"

"Shut up!" Luis yanked a baton out of his pocket and swung at my head.

I jumped back.

Wolf growled and tackled him, wresting away the club. Luis' hat fell off and I snatched it up. Turned inside out, it had a pair of fake sheep ears sewn onto the top.

Muffet had the cuffs out faster than you could say *spider*. "That's the murder weapon—it's the end of Bo Peep's crook. Luis Nimble, you're under arrest for three counts of first degree homicide."

I backed off and let Wolf and Muffet figure out the rest. It wasn't hard. Soon as Wolf showed his teeth real close to Luis' face and Muffet threatened to get a candle for his big toe, he confessed the whole thing.

They released Baa and I had to pry him off me after his fifth round of hugs and thanks for getting him out. It was just my job, and I'd do the same for any of my friends.

I offered to buy him a drink, but in the end, we both decided we'd had enough pumpkin beer for a while, so we went out for lunch instead.

BUZZ

The queen wore yellow. The court balked, garbed in stately black. Such defiance of tradition!

"How dares't thou?" hissed the regent.

The queen hummed. Buzzed, even.

The regent stepped back, too late.

The queen unfolded herself, a swarm of bees, yellow for the court's black.

PURPLE

3F313A, Threef for short, scuttled along the corridor, its CPU filled with nervous static.

Would the new purples like it? Would it be welcomed into the Shades? So often, no one saw it.

It paused by the creche door. Tapped a hesitant tentacle on steel.

The door opened and a huge banner hung from the ceiling.

WELCOME TO THE SHADES, 3F313A!

All the purples swarmed around Threef and welcomed it home.

RED

Never summon a demon on an empty stomach. It sucks and the results are questionable.

Instead of a raging, blood-red horror from the pit of hell, ready to unleash havoc upon my enemies, the thing on my carpet was more like dried-blood-red, grouchy, and the size of my fist.

"Are you Anger?" I asked. "Here to decimate those who've wronged me?"

"Nope, I'm Hangry," it responded. "Got anything to eat around here?" Then it broke my favorite lamp and trundled into the kitchen.

I sighed and made us lunch. Next time I'd plan better.

SUMMONED

It was an honest mistake. The label of the razzmatazz crayon was torn in places; the child was learning how to read.

When Ra'mat'as rose from the deeps, summoned by the human's toddler song, it was greeted with a bright purple-pink drawing of itself, offered with grape juice.

Ra'mat'as accepted the juice box and sat down to draw alongside the toddler.

ETERNAL PAPER BIRDS

The nightingale clasped the rose throne between her claws, the sharp tip hovering over her breast. Once she pierced her heart, her willingly shed blood would transform the colorless white rose into brilliant, love-hued red, and the young scholar would at last win over the object of his desire—

"Nevermore!"

The screech startled the nightingale so badly she fell off the rose tree, and was forced in an ungainly flutter of wings to catch herself before she crashed into the garden bed.

A huge black raven swooped down and landed on the path beside her. "Girl," the raven croaked, "what the hell are you doing?"

The nightingale ruffled her feathers, outraged at this interruption of her lovingly prepared sacrifice. "He pines for the woman of his dreams, and she wants only a red rose to—"

"Bullshit," the raven said, and the nightingale gasped.

Never was such coarse language used in the poems of lovelorn minstrels and consumption-plagued waifs. It was uncourtly, uncouth, unfitting.

"Look," the raven said.

From a satchel slung across his chest, he produced what appeared to be a paper-thin book, yet it had no fluttering pages nor leather-bound cover, and smelled nothing like the floral inks and delicate perfumes the nightingale was so familiar with. She had watched young lovers exchange wistful notes and longing glances in the gardens. There was a decided absence of ravens here, too.

"This Wilde guy, he's kind of an asshole to you," the raven said. He flicked one toe across the book, and a pale light shone from the single page. "All in the name of 'irony' or whatever. Look. This is you."

The nightingale peered in amazement at the words printed in a delicate, neat hand. It *was* her—her story. How she, witnessing the young scholar who yearned for a woman above his station, decided to paint a white rose red with her heart's blood so he might offer the bloom to the lady and thus win her affection.

"First of all," the raven said, "killing yourself for a flower is a little extreme."

"It's an act of love and sacrifice," the nightingale said huffily.

Although once she started to think it through, it did seem a little extreme. There were red roses a few gardens over, even if they were more pink and yellow than the white variety here. And she knew an artist who mixed delightfully vibrant paints. Maybe the whole piercing her breast with a thorn and dyeing the petals crimson had been a bit...hasty?

"Yeah, well, it doesn't even work out. Look here."

The nightingale peered at the magical paper. The story—her story—went on after her ultimate sacrifice: the scholar brought the rose to his lady, and she sneered at it. Sneered! She had already received precious gems from a different suitor, and she had no real want for a common rose, whatever its color.

"What the fuck," the nightingale whispered (for even a courtly bird such as she had learned the raw words and rather pleasing taste of profanity), outraged. She sensed the truth in the words the raven showed her.

The raven bobbed his head. "I'm from a different poem," he said, "but honestly, when it comes to humans, I'm never surprised when they're assholes."

The nightingale continued reading this Wilde author's depiction of her (now forgotten with the red rose she was supposed to die for), of the young scholar, and how he returned to his logic and forsook romantic intention and love.

"I died for nothing?" the nightingale exclaimed.

"That's why I stopped you," the raven said. "You don't deserve to be a martyr for metaphor, trapped on a page like that forever."

"Let me see this." The nightingale took the magic book—an e-ink tablet, was what the raven called it—and flicked through the endless scroll of words.

There were so many stories and poems of dying women, of sacrificed birds, or wilted roses, of dead hounds. She glared at the screen.

"With all their brains," the nightingale sputtered, "humans can't imagine us living?"

"Silly, right?" said the raven. "It's a lot of work for one bird, even one as persistent as myself. What do you say we go intervene in some other stories?"

The nightingale looked up at the white rose tree, and thought the flowers looked rather drab and tiresome now. Even if a lady wanted a red rose, there were shops not that far away. Humans were resourceful. They could figure it out.

The nightingale handed the raven his tablet back. "Whereto first?"

"Well, there's this yellow dog I think we ought to pay a visit to," said the raven.

The nightingale nodded, spread her wings, and side-by-side with the raven, she flew away to intervene elsewhere, leaving the young scholar to figure his own shit out form then on.

APPLES

"It's bitter," said the girl with skin whiter than snow , curling her perfect red lip at the apple.

"It's a Granny Smith," the witch said in exasperation. "It's sweet!"

"I dunno, tastes bad to me. Plus it's green. Is it even ripe?"

"Fine," the witch snapped, and took out a juicy red fruit. "Try this one."

MAIL ORDER

Thing about goo is that it gets fricking everywhere. In your socks, on your skin, between your eyebrow hairs.

That jungle green slime spreads and oozes and bubbles and you just can't get rid of it!

This is the last time you're ever ordering "never-ending goo!" from a catalog.

HOW GRANDMA SAVED THE WORLD AND INVENTED INTERGALACTIC DIPLOMACY

Grandma was the first person to encounter the aliens, and because of that, we're alive decades later and I get to tell you the story of how she saved the world.

It goes like this.

Grandma always believed in being kind. She talked to her potted gardenias when she watered them. She fed all the neighborhood's strays. She made tea for anyone who came to visit. She donated a check to the local foodbank once a month and volunteered on weekends.

You could say Grandma never met a living being she didn't like. She petted the grass and chatted to the local oak trees in her front yard. She apologized to the front step if she tripped on it bringing in groceries. She left crumbs in one corner of the pantry for the ants and always kept fresh water in the bird bath and nectar in the hummingbird feeders.

Maybe you think no one could be this perfect. Maybe

you think I'm exaggerating Grandma's legacy, because of how she saved the world.

Let me tell you, Grandma wasn't perfect by a long shot. She got mad at politics and she cursed so blue the dictionary ran out of words to keep up with her. She had a record for vandalism (taking out bigoted signs on neighbor's lawns), she'd been arrested for obstruction (public protests), and for assault (she punched out a douchebag while escorting a scared young woman to a clinic).

So no, Grandma wasn't a saint. But she always believed in being kind, even if sometimes you had to put politeness aside and punch a douchebag out cold.

Grandma had an open-door policy: she never locked her doors and anyone was welcome in her kitchen. Make sure you scraped off your boots if it was muddy or snowing, always say thanks when you left, and don't bother the gardenias (they have delicate dispositions).

It was December when the saucer crashed into her backyard.

Grandma had been filling up the bird feeders with seed, setting out dried ears of corn for the squirrels, and replenishing the salt lick for the deer. A tremendous BOOM! knocked her flat on her back so hard her breath huffed out in a great whoosh of steam. It wasn't thunder, even if the weather had been awfully strange--heavy clouds, electric disturbances causing power outages, and reports of weird lights in the sky.

Well, Grandma's first thought, of course, was that somebody had gotten into an accident, and she went into high gear. Grandma had taken first aid and CPR courses, and in her youth, she'd wanted to be an EMT. (She switched professions when she injured her back too badly to work in the field, and had become a public health counselor instead. She'd also worked at a crisis hotline, a Planned Parenthood clinic, and did free health seminars for endangered youth.)

Even out of breath, Grandma staggered to her feet and shuffled as fast as knee-deep snow would allow towards the sound. There wasn't any smoke, but she smelled crackling ozone and noticed her electricity was out. It was before the Winter Solstice, so days were short on light. It was near dark already, and she hurried, puffing with exertion.

The saucer had clipped one of her oak trees, which made her wince. She patted it gently in passing. She'd bandage up that gash first thing in the morning. What she focused on first was the dented metal saucer--a spaceship. Oh, yeah, Grandma loved old sci-fi movies (the original *The Day The Earth Stood Still* being her favorite) so she knew at once what had happened.

Aliens had shown up on earth!

And they were in her backyard, and their ship was damaged, and they probably needed medical attention.

The saucer's cloaking device was still flickering in and out, so it took her fifteen minutes of working up a sweat before she managed to pry down the cracked door on the ship. She'd heard weak banging on the inside, and suspected the pilot--or pilots--were trying to get out.

"Are you acclimated to our atmosphere?" Grandma called. "Or do you have appropriate hazard suits? Oh lordy, I do hope your universal translators are working. Hold on, I'm coming!"

The hatch was ajar, but she couldn't get enough

leverage with just her mitten-wrapped hands. She'd left a shovel by the garden fence to clear a path to the salt lick, so she grabbed that and used it as a pry bar. The handle snapped. But she'd done enough, and the hatch creaked open at last.

Grandma stepped back, watching with concern. There were four aliens: they didn't resemble gray bobble-headed UFO pilots or green lizard-like bipeds or tentacled atrocities, of course. They were willowy humanoids with metallic skin and six eyes and folded wings along their backs.

(Of course, we know them now as the Angels, given that most of the population still can't pronounce their proper name, but they don't mind. Some are rather flattered by the comparison to mythology.)

Two of the aliens supported a third. Even with no experience with their physiology Grandma could see right away that one was hurt. The fourth stepped forward and flared hir wings.

Grandma smiled, her stomach pitter-pattering in nervousness, and held out her arms. "Welcome to Earth! Do you require medical attention? Please come in. My house is right there. I'm not sure I have food that will meet your dietary requirements but you are more than welcome to anything in the fridge. And if you can drink tea, I'm happy to make a pot."

The first Angel slowly lowered hir wings and blinked. Then ze said, haltingly in English, "You are not hostile?"

"Me?" Grandma said, and laughed. "Oh hell no. I believe everyone deserves dignity, respect, and happiness. I try my best to live to these ideals, hard though it is some days."

It was more effusive a greeting than she normally was wont to give, but she wanted to be sure, right out of the gate, that the visitors understood her intentions and her heart.

"Detecting no lies," said the Angel. (Grandma would later learn this was the diplomatic liaison, who was an empath.)

"May I invite you inside? It's frigging cold out here, at least to a human body." Grandma pointed at her house. "I've a spare bedroom made up, and a recliner in the living room, and I might even have that old air mattress still...Come in, please." She backed towards her house, beckoned, and then held the door open as the for Angels glided across the snow and ducked into her kitchen.

She put on a pot of tea, broke out her first aid kit, and set a plate of sugar cookies on the table for her guests. She wasn't the greatest baker, truth be told, but she could make a mean pre-packaged tray of cookies right out of the fridge. She'd had two platters wrapped in foil and ready to take down for the town hall meeting.

The two Angels laid the third on the recliner in the living room and held their hands together over hir body. It wasn't so much blood as it was a discoloration along the abdomen. Grandma suspected internal bleeding, or the equivalent in their biology.

"Can I do anything to help?" she asked.

"Light, if you may spare it," said the liaison.

"I'm afraid the power's out, but the stove's gas and I have plenty of candles and an old battery powered lantern in the laundry room."

She set to work bringing light to her cheerful home. She told the gardenias about her visitors ("They seem like very nice people, and I do hope their friend is okay.") and made sure Maxie the cat was aware of the guests so he wouldn't freak out (poor thing was always nervous with new people) and told her internet modem not to stress that it couldn't get signal. The power would be back up in a while.

Grandma didn't show it, but she was still nervous. Guests! Not from Earth! It was altogether quite a shock. A pleasant one, but still...she was getting on in her years and she still had two care packages to make before the post came tomorrow. She worried she wouldn't be able to be a proper host, especially if the visitors were night owls. She tended to go to bed right around nine p.m. these days.

Once the house was as bright as she could safely make it, she stood in the kitchen and fiddled with her hands. The trio in the living room were exactly as she had left them: two holding hands over the third, whose eyes were closed.

The fourth Angel settled at the kitchen table and accepted a cup of tea. Angels have mouths very much human-like, and ze nodded in approval. It was just boxed Earl Grey, but Angels had never had earth tea before. Grandma had always believed tea could solve many problems, or at least make dealing with them easier.

The liaison finally said, "Are you the representative of this world?"

Grandma considered her reply carefully. She could be honest and say that no one person could represent an entire world populated by billions of individuals. She could give an expected answer: no, but here is a list of people who are, theoretically, in charge of running the place. (That wouldn't do at all. Grandma was mighty displeased with the current government.)

And here's the other thing about Grandma: she didn't need false modesty or self-depreciation. She knew she was a decent human. Not the best, and she had her flaws, but fundamentally, she was a good woman. She'd tried to live her life well, to give back to others, to show hospitality and compassion, to leave this Earth just a fraction better than she found it.

So she thought: why shouldn't she be a representative for Earth? Surely she couldn't speak for everyone. But right now, she was speaking just for her little corner of the world: her plot of land, the plants, the cats, the neighbor girl who brought her muffins on Sunday mornings, the deer in the back woods, herself.

"I am," she said. "One of many."

The Angel tilted hir head down in what Grandma took to be a polite gesture. "We thank you for your hospitality. Our Queen was injured in the crash. Ze will take several days to heal. May we reside here until our fleet arrives?"

"Of course," Grandma said. "You can stay as long as you like." She was honored they wanted to rest in her little house. That would give her time to settle, and to chat, and maybe Maxie would warm up to the Angels and come out to say hi.

If there was one thing Grandma loved, it was making new friends.

Grandma wouldn't know it until the power came back on and her TV and internet worked again, but all over the world, bigger saucer ships were hovering over cities and oceans. Waiting for signal from the downed craft in Grandma's back yard.

When the Angel Queen recovered, and enjoyed Grandma's famous chocolate chip pancakes, Grandma and the liaison sat down to discuss global treaties, trade relationships, and travel routes to and from Earth.

Grandma was invited up into the mothership, where she put world leaders in their place the moment anyone suggested weapons, tactics, or being an asshole to the aliens. Grandma had never been shy about talking over men. (Remember that time she punched a guy? Yep. She did it again, and this time she got applause.)

And of course, she was now best friends with the Queen, who was inclined to take Grandma's word for what would and wouldn't be good for earth. (*Yes* to better tech and advanced farming and the eradication of poverty and disease and hunger; *no* to weapons and space-travel just yet. Wait a few decades, Grandma suggested. Let humanity work through its issues on land before taking to the stars, even supervised.)

It could have been a very different story, you know. But you've seen those--the ones about war and conquest and invasion. Fictions we won't have to live. We didn't get that future because Grandma showed our friends kindness and invited strangers into her home during a time of need.

That's how Grandma saved the world: with compassion, a plate of cookies, and mugs of tea.

KAIJU

"Really?" asked God. "You want to be…green."

"Lime green!" chirruped the tiny monster. "So I can darken and grow over time, rich with algae and rot, and rise from the ocean bogs in radioactive terror to spew vengeance upon my enemies!"

"…done," said God, and Godzilla beamed.

SKY

When you think about the sky—that blue-reflected screen between you and the void—it's hard to hold it all in your head.

It's so BIG. You've never liked big problems.

You construct a vacuum. Compress the sky.

Now there's only void and that sky is the least of your problems.

LIPSTICK

The clerk lied to me.

When I said I wanted "ocean blue lipstick", to match my hair, I just accepted the little tube painted with foam-capped waves and went home.

I opened the lipstick and out poured an ocean, blue as can be. Now I'm stuck on a raft waiting for rescue.

Dammit.

MECHANIC

The robot was robin's egg blue, tiny, and didn't work.

Darcy bit her lip. What had she done wrong? She'd followed all the instructions: built it exactly right.

"Please be ok," she said, and a tear dripped onto the robot's head.

It turned on. "I am," it said.

Darcy smiled.

THE ANDROID'S PREHISTORIC MENAGERIE

The world explodes.

Unit EX-702 comes back online when UV wavelengths activate its solar plating. Its optics are crusted with red dust; a low-powered system scan concludes that though its left arm is missing and there is excessive oxidation damage along its chassis and helmet, as well as a web spun from several arachnids (*Nephila clavipes*) now embedded in its servo stump, EX-702 is functional. Its operational protocols are intact.

This unit is programmed for the support of life and sapience.

Its databanks are semi-corrupted beyond basic functions and archived footage and base knowledge dumps. Attempts to access the 'Net and reboot from a mobile hub fail with a repeated NO CONNECTION

AVAILABLE alert. EX-702 lifts its remaining arm and scrapes dust away from its optics.

Operational Function 413: this unit will maintain self-preservation operations, including but not limited to the access of immediately available data to determine procedure, when it does not conflict with the preservation of homo sapiens' *survival.*

EX-702 sits in the crater of what had been Newtonian Genetech Incorporated laboratories and HQ facility. Debris from the lab cakes the thick concrete and rusted iron walls. Its scanner matrix glitches with static-filled readouts and partially deteriorated unprocessed updates from microseconds before it was shut down.

Scientist voices agitated and unmodulated without appropriate safety masks. [STATIC] "—find survivors! Protect yourself!" [SHUT DOWN]

Something crackles against EX-702's knee joints. Fibers, synthetic and organic—old HAZMAT suits shredded and woven around broken plywood and stripped copper wiring—shaped in a non-geometric design. Inside the structure sit three maroon and heather-brown eggs thirteen centimeters in length and six in diameter.

Processing...

The eggs do not match any current avian, insectoid, reptilian, mammalian, or amphibian entries in its database. EX-702 examines the nest, which has intersected its knees. A ripped arm from the hazmat suit is tucked between its clawed toes. EX-702 is a humanoid bipedal digitigrade design with backward jointed knees and toe digits designed to grip uneven surfaces and manipulate hostile terrain. Its hand is fully articulated to mimic the human opposable thumb and fingers. EX-702 is not designed to be a nest for unknown biological organisms.

One of the eggs twitches and a small chirrup escapes the cracked calcium carbonate structure.

EX-702 reaches to remove the nest from its legs when the egg splinters and a membrane-covered nose pokes out.

Processing...

The other eggs crackle. Tiny claws, pointed snouts, wet feathers in muted brown and scarlet emerge. As the organisms free themselves, EX-702 scans them again and this time finds pictorial references in its database: *Deinonychus antirrhopus*. An extinct species of dinosaur whose fossil record suggested it would grow up to three-point-four meters as a mature adult.

There are no data points to conclude how the *Deinonychus antirrhopus* has populated once more. Newtonian Genetech Incorporated specialized in advanced human and cybernetic enhancement, for which EX-702 was a research assistant android and personal defense unit for Doctor Urashami.

The newborn trio of deinonychuses chirp and growl. EX-702 scans them. They require protein intake. A parental unit must be in the vicinity.

With UV wavelengths recharging its internal power supply and emergency batteries, EX-702 scans the area once more.

Four meters away, an adult female *Deinonychus antirrhopus* lies prone in congealing blood. Behind it sprawls the corpse of a dire wolf (*Canis dirus*). Both specimens are mauled and exhibit defensive and offensive wounds. EX-702 extrapolates that the wolf attempted to raid the nest and the female deinonychus protected her brood.

Her eyes glimmer and EX-702 stares back.

The female deinonychus growls. A staccato sound not unlike vibrating steel chords in a guitar. EX-702 does not have reference files to decode the linguistic message, but its emotive processors still work. There is desperation in the dying female's speech.

Protect.

The adult deinonychus shivers and goes still. Her heat signature begins to degenerate.

EX-702 looks down again at the hatchlings.

This unit will provide for the new life forms.

It is the custom of sapient species to identify members of a brood. Names were the most common method employed by Doctor Urashami, who christened EX-702. Doctor Urashami is the principal researcher in the cybernetic AI advancement wing of Newtonian Genetech Incorporated, and she built EX-702 herself; she often nicknamed it Seven in conversation.

The newborn raptors peer intently at EX-702. It runs a search in Names: Mythological: Alphabetical. From the results, it picks three it has records of Doctor Urashami having used.

This unit names you Andromeda, this unit names you Anubis, this unit names you Atropos.

It touches a finger to each hatchling's skull as it christens them. Its brood hisses in what EX-702 interprets as acceptance. It is now their parental unit.

It disentangles itself from the nest with precise care, its servos and wiring creaky with disuse, and accesses protocols for the processing of meat. There are two corpses available to feed its brood until it can explore the area more fully and maintain a steady supplement of nourishment for the tiny life forms in its charge.

EX-702 has no immediate data of the whereabouts or status of Doctor Urashami, so it makes a hierarchal protocol list: it will provide for its brood and it will find Doctor Urashami.

With its battery recharged, EX-702 gains access to a prime directive protocol installed by Doctor Urashami from a remote hub shortly before its initial shutdown.

Search for and assist any human survivors.

It does not find any survivors within a mile radius of the former lab. It will continue its search.

Within three months, EX-702 has established its territory of three-point-nine square acres of city ruin. The landscape has been overrun with flora formerly extinct for millions of years. Old skyscrapers are choked with huge vines and ferns. Doctor Urashami's favorite cafe, The Creme de la Bean, is a garden of semitransparent flowers and the calcified skeletons of the humans.

When hunting for its brood—migration patterns of herbivore and omnivore species crossed at the edge of EX-702's territory where a river once called the Mississippi, now three times its former size, cuts the city ruins in half— EX-702 discovered a military bunker filled with mummified human remains, a working diesel-powered generator, and a laptop with video records of the pinnacle extinction event.

Unidentified space debris penetrated the Earth's atmosphere and began what one news report described as "spinning back the world's biological clock." Prehistoric fauna and flora overwhelmed the continental landmasses; bacterial and viral infections annihilated the human population. New species thought extinct emerged from rapid evolutionary synthesis.

The records did not give enough statistical analysis to fully account for the devastation of nonorganic structural architecture, but a Lieutenant Bela Strovherd recorded an entry that EX-702 chose to save to its hard drives.

"Whoever's seeing this? Yeah, uh, welcome to the end of the world, I guess. Look, I know it's too much to hope you'll be able to find any of my family or friends and tell them..." She rubs a hand over her face, then laughs. Her voice cracks. "If you can see this, I have one request. Live. Rebuild. I think it's just time for the human race to pass the torch to whoever comes next, you know? But it'd be nice if you could remember us. We accomplished a lot of shit, but we had some good moments. I dunno. I guess...I'd just like to know someone, somewhere out there remembers. Hopefully you do better. I wish you the best, okay? I really do. Everyone here thinks I'm nuts because I'm so 'calm'"—fingers made into air quotes—"but really I'm fucking terrified. I just want to try and go out with dignity, with peace. Maybe, whoever you are, you'll see this and think, 'You know, she's not so bad.' And maybe you'll remember my face for a little while, and my voice, and my name. It's Bela, by the way. Actually named for that actor who played Dracula ages ago." A shaky smile. The camera wobbles as the room around her shakes. "Look, I'm gonna go now. I don't want you to have to

see...whatever comes next." She breathes in deep, smiles at the camera. *"Live well, okay? Maybe we'll see each other in another life."*

The video ends.

EX-702 is the last android, and androids, it has concluded, are not meant to exist in this world any longer. EX-702 does not know where it belongs now. So it watches the videos of Lieutenant Strovherd over again every night, to remember her as she asked.

Andromeda races through the Nest, her feathers brilliant red and gold. She's the largest of the three, sleek and agile, and she leads the hunting expeditions now with her sisters.

EX-702 refines the wrench head as it inserts the newly retrofitted arm into its shoulder socket. Anubis, the smallest of the brood, helps support the arm with her articulated hands.

Unit, Andromeda says, the affectionate term the raptors have called EX-702 since their birth. *Look what we found!*

The raptors speak in guttural clicks and growls. EX-702 has learned their natural language in addition to teaching them how to understand human dialects.

Atropos, whose feathers are umber and maroon like her mother's, holds out a glistening egg the size of her skull that is wrapped in heavy leather scraps. *It fell from the sky in fire, it was covered in ash.*

EX-702 scans the egg, and its heat signature exceeds one hundred Fahrenheit. *It does not appear to be of a species we have encountered.*

Andromeda clicks her sickle-claws against the cement, her neck ruff bristling in excitement. *I heard it, Unit,* she says, *I heard it burning.*

Can I see? Anubis asks.

EX-702 tightens its new arm into place and nods.

The three raptors examine the new egg, their heads flicking side to side in staccato movements. It is moments like this EX-702 thinks of Doctor Urashami's jittery hands and how she would always gesture when she talked.

Put it in the incubator, EX-702 says. *We will monitor it.*

As it watches its daughters carefully lay the egg in one of the generator-powered incubators and hover with fascination around the tank, EX-702 experiences what Doctor Urashami related as pride: it has raised Andromeda, Anubis, and Atropos into mature, successful adults. All three can hunt and build and tinker with machinery scavenged from around the city. Anubis is building an exoskeleton for advanced exploration; Andromeda is collecting paper books and printed ceramic mugs with slogans and pictures; Atropos has begun the repair on the observatory telescope.

EX-702 has still not found Doctor Urashami.

The egg hatches into a phoenix, which Anubis names Arrow of Heaven.

REPLAY: *[Lieutenant Bela Strovherd] Live well, okay? Maybe we'll see each other in another life.*

PROTOCOL: *This unit is programmed for the support of human life.*

REPLAY: *[Doctor Urashami] Hello, EX-702. Welcome to the first day of the rest of your life! Ha, always wanted to say that to someone. I'm Renee Urashami, professor of advanced robotics. Do you know why you're online? I made you to help us make the world a better place. Can't wait to see what we can accomplish!*

EX-702 finds a flash drive in Doctor Urashami's apartment, now overgrown in moss and brilliant orange mushrooms that sing ethereal music to lure prey. EX-702 is immune to the auditory and cognitive hypnosis, but it has warned its daughters of the dangerous flora and they stay away from the mushroom sector.

On the drive is an audio file labeled FOR SEVEN.

EX-702 plugs it into its USB port and listens.

AUDIO FILE: *[Doctor Urashami] Seven, I hope you find this. When I built you, I made sure you were constructed from the best materials on the planet. I wanted you to survive. But I've been thinking. I don't know if you made it out of the lab. I wasn't there when the explosion happened. I saw it on the news before we lost all signal. I can't get there in time to manually do this, but I realized that I made a mistake. I never gave you a way out. What if you're the only thing that survives? You were built to understand and develop empathy, emotional simulation. You need other people around to function, like any of us do. I have this horrifying image of you wandering a wasteland that was once Earth and finding no one, wandering until even your power cells deplete and you are alone with no understanding why. So if you find this, and there are no humans left alive, I am initiating voice-activated protocol 815: Unit EX-702 will shut down within one day of downloading this program if it has not identified human sentient life within that time frame. I do this for you, Seven. You don't deserve to be alone. I hope you forgive me.* [END FILE]

[PROGRAM 815_endprocedure *downloaded. Installing. Installation complete. Countdown: 23:59:59.*]

Unit, what's wrong? Atropos asks.

EX-702 stands by the observatory dome, a cracked sliver of dusty glass and steel, and the newly refurbished telescope within. Atropos swivels her head in curiosity.

This unit has been ordered by its creator to shut down.

[Time until shutdown: 15:25:49]

Atropos hisses and lays a clawed hand on EX-702's shoulder. *Why would she do that? You have done nothing wrong.*

Doctor Urashami did not want this unit to be alone.

The doctor is a rusted socket wrench! Atropos swears. *I do not like the humans I have seen records of.*

EX-702 watches Arrow of Heaven trace fiery tails in the sky as she learns to fly higher and higher. Anubis will be watching from the ground, her flight-capable exoskeleton still in prototype design.

Some were good, EX-702 says. It thinks of Lieutenant Bela Strovherd.

What can we do, Unit?

It has already tried to alter the downloaded program, but it has been blocked by buried subroutines and other programs activated by Doctor Urashami's virus.

Unknown. EX-702 looks at its daughter. *But I do not want to shut down.*

Andromeda, Anubis, Atropos, and Arrow of Heaven wait in a semicircle around EX-702 in the Nest. The incubators hum: some hold new eggs found without parental units attached; some house infant mammals—twin saber-toothed tiger cubs, a three-legged dire wolf, a newly hatched archaeopteryx, a two-day-old cave bear cub. All the incubators are assembled with appropriate heat lamps, milk tubes, or feeders, and are soundproofed with speakers inside issuing programmed voices of EX-702, the raptors, and ambient noise from the city.

Our family grows, EX-702 says. It wants to belong to this world, but it is still the only android. Perhaps Doctor Urashami's virus is the correct procedure. This new Earth is designed for organic life. EX-702 is synthetic.

You can't go away, snarls Anubis.

I will not forgive your human, says Atropos.

[Time until shutdown: 12:31:58]

EX-702 looks at each of its children in turn. This is their world now. They will build it as they see fit; they will remember and create new memories and prosper. It wishes it could see the future its daughters create.

Andromeda paces, her head lowered in thought. *Play the message again, Unit.*

EX-702 projects it from tinny speakers located under its faceplate. It has no articulated jaw or facial contours. Its helmet is indented with round optics and a flat polished plate where a mouth would be on a *homo sapiens* face.

All three deinonychuses listen with narrowed eyes. Then Anubis's head snaps up and she bares her teeth.

Did you hear that? she asks her sisters.

Atropos hisses in agreement. Andromeda bobs her head.

Arrow of Heaven has never spoken, but she watches with interest. Her body heat helps power the incubators when she sleeps.

Arrogance should have been the doctor's name, Atropos says. *She only said "human."*

REPLAY: *Unit EX-702 will shut down within one day of downloading this program if it has not identified human sentient life within that time frame.*

If we rewrite the words in the code, Anubis says, her feathers puffing out, *you will not shut down, Unit.*

EX-702 plugs itself into the laptop console it built to help regulate the incubators in the Nest when it was not around. Anubis, the quickest and most adroit typist of the three raptors, begins hacking into the code and searching for the precise wording in Doctor Urashami's program.

[Time until shutdown: 1:15:39]

EX-702 holds Atropos's hand. It should write a goodbye, the way Doctor Urashami and Lieutenant Bela Strovherd did. But EX-702 does not have the right words. It does not want to say goodbye.

Andromeda sings softly, a lullaby she composed from all the words she has collected.

When sleep is far
And night is long
Remember this
My sweetest song
I've followed you
Through winter snow
Through summer sun and evening dew
Remember when you go to sleep
I am beside you with teeth bared bright
I'll guide you in your dreams so deep
And be there in the morning light.

[Time until shutdown: 0:45:12]

Arrow of Heaven trundles close, then pulls from beneath her glossy wing a sheet of copper, embossed with a drawing of EX-702 looking up at the night sky. The star constellations show all three raptors.

Lovely, EX-702 says. Arrow of Heaven ducks her beak in pleasure and purrs.

[INTRUDER DETECTION. ACCELERATION OF SHUTDOWN IMMINENT.]

No! Anubis cries. She tries to type faster.

Andromeda's song falters. Atropos clutches EX-702's hand tighter.

[Time until shutdown: 0:0:35]

EX-702 replays Lieutenant Bela Strovherd's clip: *Look, I'm gonna go now. I don't want you to have to see...whatever comes next.* But only in its own processor. If the last thing it sees is its family, the new world it has helped begin, then it will hold tight to that and remember even when its core goes dark.

Before the world exploded, EX-702 accompanied Doctor Urashami to a board meeting where she demonstrated EX-702's behavioral and emotional intelligence parameters. "This is the future of our people," she said. "No bias, no inefficiency. Pure, mechanical perfection."

EX-702 experienced the satisfying effect of pride; it had excelled in its function and pleased Doctor Urashami.

"You want to give the world to robots?" asked one of the board members.

Doctor Urashami shook her head. "When we roll out the new models, and begin the tests on human uploads and upgrades, within ten years humans will have advanced beyond anything we thought possible a decade ago. We will have no need of robots, then. We will be superior in every way."

EX-702's elation defused. It must have incorrectly interpreted Doctor Urashami's reaction to its presentation. It would run a diagnostic to find where its malfunction lay, if it as a unit was considered unnecessary.

"Good," said another of the board members. "I don't care for a future with *that*."

EX-702 was not allowed to express emotion outside of the demonstration. What would become of it when *homo sapiens* no longer had any use for an android?

In darkness, EX-702 dreams. Or, perhaps, this is death. It hears Andromeda's song like a distant echo.

EX-702 does not know what becomes of androids when they die. It hopes it will not be alone, whatever becomes of it.

It tries to keep the memory of its family bright in its processor—but the image de-pixelates, data deleted. First Andromeda, then the others disappear. Spaces where the visual should be fills with holes. EX-70 is helpless, its autonomous function superseded.

No, please let me keep this, EX-7 protests to the core-wipe program.

The shutdown does not acknowledge EX-.

The faint auditory input dissolves in static. When the memory of three deinonychuses disappears and the phoenix snuffs out, EX shudders. This, then, must be death.

The world ends.

EX-702 comes back online.

It lies in the middle of the nest, all four daughters curled next to it. Anubis blinks and stretches.

Unit! Atropos chitters, and headbutts EX-702 in the chassis the way she did as a hatchling to show her delight.

EX-702 sits up. Memory banks restore from backups, its last visual stitched together in its processor once more. *You were successful, Anubis.*

Barely! Anubis grins. *But I reworded the program and omitted all uses of the word "human." I also did a little more tweaking when you went into stasis and rebooted. I've disabled the majority of the blocks that prevented you from self-modification. You can do whatever you want now.*

Are you all right? asks Andromeda.

Yes, says EX-702. It looks at its daughters and the incubators humming inside the Nest. *Yes, I am all right.*

EX-702 wraps its arms around its daughters and watches the sun rise over their world.

TEAL

She painted the house deep teal despite complaints.

She set her caldron out in the front yard even with fines from the homeowner's association.

She posted flyers on all the telephone poles.

SCARED? HURT? CAN'T GO HOME? COME TO THE TEAL HOUSE. THE WITCH WILL KEEP YOU SAFE.

She meant every word, and a witch always keeps her promises.

DEJA VU

—as my hopper ship *Cerulean Blue* drops from orbit, I get the weirdest sense I've been here before.

Ain't possible, of course. This is uncharted territory! The world stretches out in green-gray patchwork.

A glint of silver. Another ship? I low?

I magnify the scanners.

In my viewscreen, I see my ship. *Cerulean Blue* lies crashed inside the pincers of a rocky cliff.

Impossible. I bank, but something nullifies the controls and I'm falling, gonna crash—

—as my hopper ship drops out of orbit, I get the weirdest sense I've been here before…

CURIOSITY

There's a saying among the sky-wranglers: Never touch the cobalt clouds.

Not with dawn-forged gloves or wind-braided lassos. You touch 'em and you ain't seen again.

Those cobalt spheres, drifting among cumulus, they go somewhere elsewise.

Me? I'm a cat. 'Course I'm curious.

Let's see what's on the other side.

BRAND NAME

"I don't understand," the dragon wailed. "I used the polish just like you said! I'm supposed to be a terror of the skies! I'm *pink*!"

"Show me the label." The witch sighed. "Oh, honey, this is to color your scales violet-red. Violent Red is the brand you were looking for."

"How will I ever be taken seriously now?" the dragon asked.

The witch grinned. "Honey, pink is all the rage right now. I think you'll be a massive hit with the 8-12 year old demographic."

The dragon blinked. "Really?"

The witch nodded. "You told me you wanted attention, right? That's why you dyed your scales."

The dragon examined itself: glittery pale rose pink, its sharp white claws a rather striking contrast now against the new color. "True…"

"Plus," the witch added with a grin, "you're the only pink dragon I know of, and I know them all."

The dragon's eye lit up. "You're *right*!"

"In face," the witch continued, scrolling through her phone, "I bet you'll start a trend. Want me to post a photo on my timeline?"

"Absolutely!" The dragon preened, then posed, flashing its teeth and showing off its new scale colors. "This is the best thing ever!"

MONSTERS

Dust swirled about the monster as it rumbled awake. A cough startled it and it peered through the moss growing over its brow.

A human child sat on its stoney knuckles, holding a book. "Sorry—"

"Forgiven," the monster said. "Will you read to me?

"Yes!"

DEVIL

The Devil went down to Georgia but it wasn't for a soul to steal. Really, the Devil just wanted to fulfill a random dream he'd had: to make a cameo as one of the zombies on the final season of *The Walking Dead*.

Of course, a few extra souls wouldn't hurt. It was Hollywood, after all.

FINDING HOME

The reality I was born in ceased to exist when I was three years old. So Mama and I moved to a different reality.

We moved a lot, actually.

"We can't stay more than a few years," Mama would say as she unzipped the fabric of the space-time continuum and scanned the flickering images inside.

There were so many, I got motion sick if I looked too long.

But Mama always knew which one to pick. She'd catch a corner of a shimmering image, brightly colored like rainbow sprinkles, then take my hand and pull us both through.

I met Amand in a coffee shop on a rainy day two years and nine months after my mother and I moved to this reality. The café menu offered various espressos and lattes, the

Germanized English happily familiar. I thanked the barista and looked for a seat.

That first glimpse: Amand sat in a corner, reading *Die Liebe der Bienen*, a bestseller literary graphic novel that had a different ending for everyone who read it.

Grayish afternoon light highlighted his black curly hair and dark skin, and his glasses adjusted to the light flow, the rims bright blue. Broad shoulders were highlighted under the fashionable sweater he wore, navy blue with the New Chicago Physics (the local soccer team) logo emblazoned on the chest.

He flipped the last page and sighed, dark eyes half-closed in contentment.

He caught me staring at him. I was used to that by now. Odd looks when I couldn't lose my accent or maybe I had a neon sign over my head that read DOESN'T BELONG.

"What ending did you get?" I asked.

He grinned. "Dominik and Erik reconcile, and then Erik proposes and he accepts and they live well to their days' end. It's what I hoped for."

I smiled back. "That's the ending I got, too. Well. Dominik proposed, when I read it."

"Amand," he said, offering his hand.

"Joseph," I replied. We shook. My heartbeat hadn't slowed, though I had yet to sip my cappuccino. "Can I join you?"

He nodded at the plush armchair next to him. "I would like this."

Each new reality was different.

Sometimes there'd be buildings in the sky, sometimes technology was less advanced, and sometimes there wasn't anybody around at all.

(Mama picked those empty realities once in a while, but we only stayed for a few days.)

Mama had a talent for explaining who we were to the people in each reality: why we had weird clothes and accents, why our skin was the color it was, sometimes why I was a boy (if they hadn't been invented yet), sometimes why she was a girl, and sometimes why we had genders at all.

She had a gift. She knew which realities were unsafe. She could make people like us, or at least not hate us. She was extraordinary but she never drew attention. Mama designed new cover stories depending on where we ended up. Mama never had trouble understanding the language. She'd teach me, but I didn't have her skill. It got harder as I got older, too, always being the weird kid.

"Don't make friends you can't let go of, Joseph," Mama always said. "We can't stay long."

"Why not?" I asked angrily when I was ten. I'd just met Mohamed who lived down the street, and he was going to let me drive his custom-built racecar.

"Because our atoms don't belong here," Mama said, "and eventually we'll crumble into little pieces if we stay too long. Reality-bending is tricky."

So I didn't have many friends. I knew people, lots of people, but they were a sea of changing faces and bodies and names (or sometimes numbers).

I tried not to let Mama know I was lonely. We had to survive. She was trying to make a good life for us.

And she'd promised that one day we'd find Daddy again.

Amand and I spent the next two months inseparable. He showed me the old baroque district, full of niche clubs and piano halls and statues of composers and artists and philosophers. We toured the Babylon Gardens, reconstructed and raised half a mile into the sky.

I was nineteen. I'd been in and out of so many schools I wasn't sure what level my education qualified. Amand had just finished college. He was applying for jobs in the energy reconstruction projects, striving for cleaner power and more of it. New Chicago was prospering, but so much of the continent was still ravaged from the Fallout War, reconstruction and rehabilitation for the country was slow.

Amand wanted to help change that, the determination clear in every fluid movement, in the line of his jaw, in the brightness of his eyes. I couldn't keep my eyes off him when we were together. I didn't want to.

I didn't want to fall in love. Or maybe I did. It was so hard to tell.

"You're moody today, mein Herz," Amand said, rubbing his thumb over my knuckles. We held hands and leaned on the railing atop the new hydroelectric dam. It wasn't technically open to tourists yet, but he'd snuck in before— his aunt was the foreman and the workers liked him—and told me this was the most stunning view of the sunrise you could see outside of the tower complexes. "What is wrong?"

I shrugged. "I have to move soon."

God, I'd told him when we first went out that I wasn't going to be in town for more than a few months. It was my mother's work schedule, I'd explained, and I accompanied her because she had health concerns. (The lies had been harder than ever before, stuck like congealed oatmeal in my throat.)

I was so tired of moving. But what choice did we have? Move, or cease to exist.

"But you don't want to," Amand said slowly.

I gazed down at the polished curve of the dam. It was a long way down, even with the safety nets strung at intervals across the face. "Nein," I whispered. "I like it here."

Amand slung an arm over my shoulders. "There is no one else who could take care of her while she travels?"

Mom didn't need my help. I needed hers. How long would it continue? Until she died from an accident or old age? Since I didn't know how to unzip the space-time continuum, I'd be stuck facing my inevitable death somewhere that wasn't home. Alone.

The depressive realization hit like I'd swallowed an old, bitter espresso shot. Dizziness swamped my head and I pushed away from the railing before I lost my balance or puked. Armand's arm steadied me.

The nippy wind tousled his hair and snaked down my collar. It was still dark, our only illumination the safety lights down the curvature of the dam.

"I can't leave her," I said. The first red bars of dawn

peeked over the horizon, backlighting the uneven cityscape's profile.

Amand's expression was unreadable. "Well," he said at length, "we can always write or vidchat, and you can visit again, ja?"

But I couldn't, so I only nodded. I rubbed my face. The wind had made my eyes water.

He was right, though. The sunrise view from the dam was amazing.

My second favorite reality was where I met Dr. Amelia D'Cruz. Mom dated her briefly while we integrated into the tropical cities spread like a beaded bracelet around the equator.

I was six, and Mom had promised me she would look for a doctor who could perform gender reassignment surgery for me. It took her slightly longer not to call me Josephine, but only a little.

Dr. Amelia smelled like bubblegum and cinnamon, and she always smiled so bright that I wanted to smile back.

I told Mom I didn't want to leave when, almost three years to the day—my surgery two years past—we packed our bags and said goodbyes.

I clung to Dr. Amelia, who rubbed my back and kept saying, "It's okay, Joseph. You'll find a place you belong one day. You'll find your home. I promise."

I didn't believe her, and I didn't speak to Mom for days after we stepped into a new reality and started over yet again.

"It's time to go, Joseph," Mom said. We sat eating noodles and watching the news that same evening. "We have to leave tomorrow."

I set my bowl down, my stomach heavy. How had time gone by so fast? I thought I had another week left with Amand.

"Are you sure?" I asked.

She fiddled with her chopsticks. Her gaze remained on the screen. "We've been here too long. There's nothing for us."

"What?" That wasn't her usual explanation. She would tell me of the destabilization in her bones, the static buzz in her sinuses that told her we were getting close.

"He's not here," she said.

Dad had disappeared before I was old enough to remember. She said we'd find him and we'd discover a reality that we could live in as a family.

We'd wasted sixteen years. I didn't know what a home was, what stability was like.

All I could think of was Amand's face, his quirky smile and stuttering laugh. The way his hands felt in my hair and on my skin. How he always arrived on time. Even when his temper flared and we got into arguments about politics or history, he'd kiss me afterwards and say the way I confused the timeline was adorable, making up events in place of real ones.

(I hadn't told him that those events were real somewhere else.)

I stood up and slammed my bowl in the sink. "We're not going to find him, you know."

"He's out there somewhere," Mom said, almost to herself. "We aren't giving up on him. Pack your things."

She knew what she was looking for. She had always known.

I didn't know what he looked like, let alone what kind of man he was. She never told me stories; maybe she didn't want me to grieve for something I might never have.

I thought of Amand and how he always wore mismatched socks and programmed his glasses frames to match his shirts. Did I even know what I wanted?

I'd always been focused on not growing too attached, on being able to leave everything behind. It felt like I'd grown up a hundred times and then fallen down the ladder to land back where I'd started, never knowing when it would stop.

Would I ever have what she had with my father, if I always left before I could find out?

Mom put a hand on my shoulder. She had to reach, now. "It won't be forever, Joey."

I covered her hand with mine.

I was so tired of running and never getting anywhere. It had to stop.

"I know," I said. "That's why I'm not leaving."

I turned around in time to see her bite her lip.

"Nonsense," she said, but without conviction.

I held her hand tight. "I can't do this anymore. I want to stay here, with Amand"—if he would keep me—"even if it's dangerous."

"But..." She took several deep breaths. Arguing with herself. Finding excuses, reasons, commands. Her shoulders slumped. "You're grown up, aren't you? Not my little boy anymore."

"I'll always be your son, Mom. But I need to do this for myself. I need something to call my own."

She blinked hard. "You won't have much time. A few weeks at most. Please just come with me. We'll find your father—"

"No," I said gently. "A little time's better than having forever with nothing to show for it." That was one of Amand's favorite quotes from *Die Liebe der Bienen*.

What if she was right and I disintegrated once the three years were up?

Was that really worth hurting Amand? Or was it any different than stepping out of this reality, out of his life, forever?

"Please, Mama." I kissed her hand. "I need to stay."

She pulled me into a hug. Her body trembled. "Let me show you how to unzip the fabric," she whispered. "So you have a way out."

"No," I said into her hair. I wanted to be like the people around me, given one life to make what they would of it. "I'll take my chances."

I asked Amand to come with me to see my mother off the next day. I didn't know where she was headed.

We stood in a dry field outside the city limits as Mom unzipped the space-time continuum. Amand gripped my arm as we watched.

She held out her hand once to me, but I shook my head.

"Bye, Mom," I said.

She didn't say goodbye. Maybe she couldn't.

She took hold of a corner of another reality and pulled herself through. Then she was gone, and the seam melted closed.

I sagged against Amand.

Mom wasn't here. That sudden emptiness hit me harder than any reality-hop. My knees buckled.

He caught me and held me.

I didn't know I could miss her so badly so fast.

"What if I never see her again?" I said into Amand's chest.

The rims of his glasses pressed against my temple. "We always find our family." Then, softly, "Will you stay with me?"

"Ja," I said. "As long as I can."

I felt him smile.

I haven't seen my mother in ten years.

Amand and I got married. We adopted two beautiful children—Monique and Sebastian—and we've been living each day as if it's the last. It might be.

But, sometimes, I don't think it will happen the way Mom predicted. I don't think my mother wasn't entirely honest with me as a kid.

My dad ran off through a different reality when I was two. She waited a year, but he didn't come back. She wanted to find him the only way she knew how, and what else was she going to do with me except take me along?

Maybe the three year limit was just an arbitrary

definition because she couldn't bear to stay anywhere too long and let Dad drift father away.

I'm not angry at her. If I hadn't reality-hopped, I wouldn't have met Amand. I wouldn't have settled down in this sky apartment overlooking New Chicago, landed a job as an art historian, found a loving husband, two amazing kids, friends, and a life I'm content with. (I dedicated my first memoir to Dr. Amelia and my mom, in gratitude.)

There are days I wonder if Mom was right about our atoms not connecting with this reality we live in now. One day, I might just snap out of existence. If I do, I won't have too many regrets.

(I'd told Amand my whole story after Mom left. He believed every word. The day before he proposed a year later, I told him again about the risk I could just vanish.

"Risks are just life with different letters," he said, and kissed me. "We'll take risks and life together, ja?"

"Ja," I'd said, pulling him closer.)

If I see Mom again, the only regret I'll have is that she won't stay for very long. Wherever she is, I hope she finds what she's looking for. Me? I've found my home.

CLUBBING

The first rule of Ghost Club is don't admit you're dead.

That just kills the mood, you know?

If you must acknowledge corporality, the correct phrase is "limited physical existence."

Second rule: have fun! Carry on with life! You're dead, not entombed.

BEST FRIEND

This angel wasn't like the others. It wasn't a celestial warrior; it didn't have a trumpeting voice like the archangels; it wasn't robed in glory and didn't carry a flaming sword.

But it stuck by its human, tail wagging, heart full of love. A good dog.

The best angel there ever was.

MOVING DAY

It's hard moving to a new house in a new state when you're a kid.

You miss your friends and making new ones is hard. You sit on your bed and cry yourself to sleep the first night.

Something wakes you. You look up at the trio of monsters standing over you, and gasp.

"You guys came with?"

"Always," your monsters say, and you're not so alone now.

GOODNIGHT

"Are you sleeping?" asked The Thing In The Night.

"Yes," said the Closet Monster.

"No," said the Underbed Monster.

"Maybe," said the Branch At the Window.

"Not anymore," I whispered, and turned off the light.

AFTERWARDS

"Yo, Boney McSkullface!"

The Grim Reaper turns. "What did you call me?"

"You heard."

Grim smiles sadly at their unexpected visitor. "I didn't think you could die."

"I can't," Love says. "World's over. I'd like you to come live again. With me."

Grim hesitates.

"It's OK, pal." Love offers a lopsided grin. "Change is hard. I can wait."

Grim lays down their scythe. "No need, my friend. I'm ready."

THE GHOST

The old man always forgot where he put his keys, so the ghost found them.

The man's husband often got too warm, so the ghost adjusted the thermostat.

One day, the men set the table for three and invited the ghost to share tea.

"We noticed. Thank you."

THIS IS NOT A WARDROBE DOOR

Dear Gatekeeper,

Hi my name is Ellie and I'm six years old and my closet door is broken. My best friend Zera lives in your world and I visited her all the time, and sometimes I got older but turned six again when I came back, but that's okay. Can you please fix the door so I can play with Zera?

Love,

Ellie

Zera packs lightly for her journey: rose-petal rope and dewdrop boots, a jacket spun from bee song and buttoned with industrial-strength cricket clicks. She secures her belt (spun from the cloud memories, of course) and picks up her satchel. It has food for her and oil for Misu.

Her best friend is missing and she must find out why.

Misu, the palm-sized mechanical microraptor, perches

on her seaweed braids, its glossy raindrop-colored feathers ruffled in concern.

Misu says, *But what if the door is locked?*

Zera smiles. "I'll find a key."

But secretly, she's worried. What if there isn't one?

Dear Gatekeeper,

I hope you got my last couple letters. I haven't heard back from you yet, and the closet door still doesn't work. Mommy says I'm wasting paper when I use too much crayon, so I'm using markers this time. Is Zera okay? Tell her I miss playing with the sea monsters and flying to the moon on the dragons most of all.

Please open the door again.

Ellie, age 7

Zera leaves the treehouse and climbs up the one-thousand-five-hundred-three rungs of the polka-dot ladder, each step a perfect note in a symphony. When she reaches the falcon aerie above, she bows to the Falcon Queen and asks if she may have a ride to the Land of Doors.

The Falcon Queen tilts her magnificent head. "Have you not heard?" asks the queen in a voice like spring lightning and winter calm. "All the doors have gone quiet. There is a disease rotting wood and rusting hinges, and no one can find a cure."

Misu shivers on Zera's shoulder. *It is like the dreams,* Misu says. *When everything is silent.*

Zera frowns. "Hasn't the empress sent scientists to investigate?"

The Falcon Queen nods. "They haven't returned. I dare not send my people into the cursed air until we know what is happening."

Zera squares her shoulders. She needs answers, and quickly. Time passes differently (faster) on Ellie's home planet, because their worlds are so far apart, and a lag develops in the space-time continuum.

"Then I will speak to the Forgotten Book," Zera says, hiding the tremor in her voice.

The falcons ruffle their feathers in anxiety. Not even the empress sends envoys without the Forgotten Book's approval.

"You are always brave," says the Falcon Queen. "Very well then, I will take you as far as the Island of Stars."

Hi Gatekeeper,

Are you even there? It's been almost a year for me and still nothing. Did the ice elves get you? I hope not. Zera and I trapped them in the core of the passing comet so they'd go away, but you never know.

Why can't I get through anymore? I'm not too old, I promise. That was those Narnia books that had that rule (and they were stupid, we read them in class).

Please say something,

Ellie, age 8

Zera hops off the Falcon Queen's back and looks at the Island of Stars. It glows from the dim silver bubbles that thick in the air like tapioca pudding.

She sets off through the jungle of broken wire bedframes and abandoned armchairs; she steps around rusting toys and rotting books. There are memories curled everywhere — sad and lonely things, falling to pieces at the seams.

She looks around in horror. "What happened?"

Misu points with a tiny claw. *Look.*

In the middle of the island stands the Forgotten Book, its glass case shattered and anger radiating off its pages.

LEAVE, says the book. **BEFORE MY CURSE DEVOURS YOU.**

Gatekeeper,

I tried to tell Mom we can't move, but she won't listen. So now I'm three hundred miles away and I don't know anybody and all I want to do is scream and punch things, but I don't want Mom to get upset. This isn't the same closet door. Zera explained that the physical location wasn't as fixed like normal doors in our world, but I'm still freaking out.

I found my other letters. Stacks of notebook paper scribbled in crayon and marker and finger-paint — all stacked in a box in Mom's bedroom.

"What are you doing with this?" I screamed at Mom, and she had tears in her eyes. "Why did you take the letters? They were supposed to get to Zera!"

Mom said she was sorry, she didn't want to tell me to

stop since it seemed so important, but she kept finding them in her closet.

I said I'd never put them there, but she didn't believe me.

"We can't go there again," Mom said, "no one ever gets to go back!" and she stomped out of the kitchen and into the rain.

Has my mom been there? Why didn't she ever tell me? Why did you banish her too?

What did we do so wrong we can't come back?

Ellie

Zera's knees feel about to shatter.

"Why are you doing this?" Zera grips an old, warped rocking chair. "You've blacked out the Land of Doors, haven't you?"

YES, says the Book. **ALL WHO GO THERE WILL SLEEP, UNDREAMING, UNTIL THE END.**

Zera blinks hard, her head dizzy from the pressure in the air. "You can't take away everyone's happiness like this."

NO? says the Book. **WHY NOT? NO ONE EVER REMEMBERS US THERE. THEY FORGET AND GROW OLD AND ABANDON US.**

"That's not true," Zera says. "Ellie remembers. There are others."

Misu nods.

Zera pushes through the heavy air, reaching out a hand to the Book. "They tell stories of us there," Zera says, because Ellie used to bring stacks of novels with her instead of PBJ sandwiches in her backpack. "There are people who believe. But there won't be if we close all the doors. Stories in their world will dry up. We'll start to forget them, too."

WE MEAN NOTHING TO THEM.

Zera shakes her head. "That's not true. I don't want my best friend to disappear forever."

Gatekeeper,

I don't know why I bother anymore. You're not listening. I don't even know if you exist.

It's been awhile, huh? Life got busy for me. High school, mostly. Mom got a better job and now we won't have to move again. Also I met this awesome girl named LaShawna and we've been dating for a month. God, I'm so in love with her. She's funny and smart and tough and kind — and she really gets me.

Sometimes she reminds me of Zera.

I asked Mom why she kept my letters.

She didn't avoid me this time. "I had a door when I was younger," she said, and she looked so awfully sad. "I was your age. I met the person I wanted to stay with forever." She let out her breath in a whoosh. "But then the door just... it broke, or something. I tried dating here. Met your father, but it just wasn't the same. Then he ran off and it was like losing it all again."

I told LaShawna about Zera's world. She said she didn't want to talk about it. I think maybe she had a door, too.

I was so angry growing up, feeling trapped. You know the best thing about Zera? She *got* me. I could be a girl, I could be a boy, and I could be neither — because that's how I feel a lot of the time. Shifting around between genders. I want that to be okay, but here? I don't know.

The thing is, I don't want to live in Zera's world forever. I love things here, too. I want to be able to go back and forth and have friends everywhere, and date LaShawna and get my degree and just *live*.

This will be my last letter to you, Gatekeeper.

If there was one thing Zera and I learned, it's that you have to build your own doors sometimes.

So I'm going to make my own. I'll construct it out of salvaged lumber; I'll take a metalworking class and forge my own hinges. I'll paper it with all my letters and all my memories. I'll set it up somewhere safe, and here's the thing — I'll make sure it never locks.

My door will be open for anyone who needs it: my mom, LaShawna, myself.

—Ell

The Book is silent.

"Please," Zera says. "Remove the curse. Let us all try again."

And she lays her hand gently on the Forgotten Book and lets the Book see all the happy memories she shared with Ellie, once, and how Ellie's mom Loraine once came here and met Vasha, who has waited by the door since the curse fell, and Misu, who befriended the lonely girl LaShawna and longs to see her again — and so many, many others that Zera has collected, her heart overfilled with joy and loss and grief and hope.

In return, she sees through space and time, right into Ell's world, where Ell has built a door and has her hand on the knob.

"Ell," Zera calls.

Ell looks up, eyes wide. "Zera?"

"Yes," Zera says, and knows her voice will sound dull behind the door. "I'm here."

Ell grins. "I can see your reflection in the door! Is that the Book with you?"

The Book trembles. **SHE REMEMBERS.**

Zera nods. The air is thinning, easing in her lungs. "I told you. Not everyone forgets."

I would like to see LaShawna again, says Misu.

VERY WELL, says the book. **THE CURSE WILL BE REMOVED.**

Ell turns the handle.

Bright lights beams into the Island of Stars, and Ell stands there in a doorway, arms spread wide. Zera leaps forward and hugs her best friend.

"You came back," Zera says.

"I brought some people with me, too," Ell says, and waves behind her, where two other women wait.

Loraine steps through the light with tears in her eyes. "I never thought I could come back..."

Misu squeaks in delight and flies to LaShawna.

Zera smiles at her friends. Things will be all right.

"We have a lot of work to do to repair this place," Zera says. She clasps Ell's hands. "The curse is gone, but we have to fix the doors and wake the sleepers. Are you ready?"

Ell grins and waves her mom and girlfriend to join her. "Yes. Let's do this."

ORIGINAL PUBLICATION INFO

"Just Like Mombeast Used to Make" first published on Patreon (2017). © Merc Fenn Wolfmoor

"Bad, Bad Black Sheep" first published on Patreon (2018). © Merc Fenn Wolfmoor

"Eternal Paper Birds" first published in *Good Monsters And Friends: Stories* (2022). © Merc Fenn Wolfmoor

"How Grandma Saved the World And Invented Intergalactic Diplomacy" first published on Patreon (2017). © Merc Fenn Wolfmoor

"The Android's Prehistoric Menagerie" first published in Mothership Zeta (2016). © Merc Fenn Wolfmoor

"Finding Home" first published in Vitality Magazine (2015). © Merc Fenn Wolfmoor

SIGN UP FOR THE NEWSLETTER!

Want to keep up-to-date with the newest releases from Merc Fenn Wolfmoor? Join their mailing list and be the first to know when a new book or collection is available. :D

Plus, get a FREE original short story when you subscribe: https://mercfennwolfmoor.com/subscribe/

ABOUT THE AUTHOR

Merc Fenn Wolfmoor is a non-binary, queer writer from Minnesota, where they live with their two cats. Merc is the author of several short story collections including *Friends For Robots* (2021), *These Imperfect Reflections* (2022), *Good Monsters and Friends* (2022), and several novellas (*The Wolf Among the Wild Hunt* and *The Wolf Against the Court of Stone*). They have had short stories published in such fine venues as Lightspeed, Nightmare, Apex, Beneath Ceaseless Skies, Escape Pod, Uncanny, and more. Visit their website: mercfennwolfmoor.com for more, or follow them on Twitter @Merc_Wolfmoor.

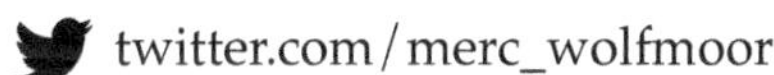 twitter.com/merc_wolfmoor

ALSO BY MERC FENN WOLFMOOR

COLLECTIONS

Friends For Robots: Short Stories

The Lawless: A Triptych

These Imperfect Reflections: Short Stories

THE SCYTHEWULF CHRONICLES

The Wolf Among the Wild Hunt

The Wolf Against the Court of Stone

[forthcoming Autumn 2022]

STAND-ALONE TITLES

Hero's Choice

ALSO FROM ROBOT DINOSAUR PRESS

SANCTUARY BY ANDI C. BUCHANAN
Morgan's home is a sanctuary for ghosts. When it is threatened they must fight for the queer, neurodivergent found-family they love and the home they've created.

FLOTSAM BY R J THEODORE
A scrappy group of outsiders take a job to salvage some old ring from Peridot's gravity-caught garbage layer, and land squarely in the middle of a plot to take over (and possibly destroy) what's left of the already tormented planet.

THE MIDNIGHT GAMES: SIX STORIES ABOUT GAMES YOU PLAY ONCE EDITED BY RHIANNON RASMUSSEN
Six frightening tales illustrated by Andrey Garin await you inside, with step by step instructions for those brave—or desperate—enough to play.

THEY DREAMED OF DEAD SHIPS BY BYRON M. KAIN
A terrifying plague sweeps the world, and there is nowhere safe…for it comes to you in a dream about a ship. And then it is too late.

A STARBOUND SOLSTICE BY JULIET KEMP
Celebrations, aliens, mistletoe, and a dangerous incident in the depths of mid-space. A sweet festive season space story with a touch of (queer) romance.

YOU FED US TO THE ROSES: SHORT STORIES BY CARLIE ST. GEORGE
Final girls who team up. Dead boys still breathing. Ghosts who whisper secrets. Angels beyond the grave, yet not of heaven. Wolves who wear human skins. *You Fed Us To the Roses* is a disturbing, visceral, triumphant collection no horror fan will want to miss.

Find these great titles and more at your favorite ebook retailer!

Visit us at: www.robotdinosaurpress.com